Edwin Longsden Long

Ione

A tale of Ephesus

Edwin Longsden Long

Ione
A tale of Ephesus

ISBN/EAN: 9783337174125

Printed in Europe, USA, Canada, Australia, Japan

Cover: Foto ©Andreas Hilbeck / pixelio.de

More available books at **www.hansebooks.com**

IONE

A TALE OF EPHESUS

By JAMES S. PARK

SUGGESTED BY EDWIN LONG'S PAINTING

"CHRIST OR DIANA"

NEW YORK
ANSON D. F. RANDOLPH & COMPANY
(INCORPORATED)
182 FIFTH AVENUE

I O N E.

I.

IN days of seedtime of the Christian
    faith,
  When men were seeking every-
    where for light,
Or clasping old traditions close, there lived
At Ephesus a venerable Greek
Called Ctesiphon. The changing years had
    left
Their grief as well as gladness in his heart;
His life-long friend, Antonius of Rome,
Coming on business ventures, year by year,
Had been persuaded, ere his last return,
To leave awhile his young son, Marius;
But midway in the voyage the treacherous
    wind

Whirled the calm ripples into angry waves,
And driving his galley hard upon the rocks,
Sunk it, with all on board. The sad news
    came
Months afterward to the Ephesian home,
And music changed to mourning. But the
    boy
Was loved and cherished by his father's
    friend,
And hardly did he know his orphanage
Till his adoption. Soon he had become
The dear companion in all pleasant hours
Of the three sisters, younger than himself,
Ione, Lesbia, and Pelope.
Gay, eager rivals were they in the search
For the first wild-flowers after winter's
    snows ;
They watched the kingly eagle, floating high,
Or wondered at the rainbow's radiant arch,
Or roaming in the dim old forest, learned
Secrets of birds and bees, of trees and
    moss ;
They sailed their mimic fleets upon the
    stream,

While sitting down, they cut long, hollow
stalks,
And breathing in them brought forth mel-
low tones ;
Or chased, with ringing laughter, playful
goats
Around the field, till flushed and out of
breath,
They sank down panting in the fragrant
grass ;
And many another pastime filled the days'
Deep chalice to the brim with sparkling
wine.

Five happy years went by on shining wings ;
Then came a change, as Marius was of age
For Roman schooling, as Antonius wished,
In eloquence, and arms, and government,
At the world's capital. Darker seemed the
house,
And dimmed the sunshine over all the land,
When he had left them, after long farewells.
Ione wandered restlessly about,
Missing her leader in a hundred ways,

Till marking how a cloud enwrapped the
  hearts
Of father, mother, sisters, even the slaves,
She strove by thoughtful, gentle ministry
To bring back smiles and gladness. Day
  by day
Their loss was lessened, and she took his
  place,
As far as might be, to depending ones.

Then letters came, as months and years
  rolled on,
Telling of progress, with a glow of pride
In deeds of ancient days, and how he
  burned
Already to be leader of a host
In some great enterprise. Ione felt
A thrill of sympathy with all his thought,
And treasured up the words like precious
  gems,
Because he wrote them.

     But a dark-browed Guest
Was daily drawing nearer to the house
Unbidden, till at length they heard a knock

Imperious, and he entered, took the hand
Of wife and mother in his chilling clasp,
And she whose life was closely twined with
    theirs,
Making one harp-string, sounding full and
    sweet,
Passed into silence, with the voiceless
    shades.
Then Ctesiphon's sad, desolated heart,
Too tender for his grim philosophy,
Would not be comforted, but wandered out
Into the darkness, asking for some strong
Assurance of an endless, unseen life,
With re-united souls, but all in vain.
Ione nobly strove again to fill
A place made vacant, but her weight of grief
Was overpowering sometimes, till she slipped
Away from all, and wept despairingly.
The younger children felt the sudden shock
Less keenly, and their spirits soon revived,
Till sunshine almost filled their restless
    hearts,
Save in the father's presence, when they
    marked

How slow his step, how sorrowful his face,
Where grief had ploughed deep furrows in
    the brow,
And scattered ashes on his hair and beard,
Until it seemed that in the space of months
Long years had passed ; instinctively they
    hushed
Their laughter then, and spoke in lower
    tones.

So the dull days crept on with folded wings ;
The sun, retreating toward the southern
    pole,
Was sometimes hid from sight by leaden
    clouds,
And chilly winds began to blow from seas
And eastern deserts, heralds of the stern
Gray monarch Winter; soon the shivering
    land
Lay bound in icy fetters, and no voice
From Nature's myriad summer tongues
    could speak
Of coming life and beauty, — all was death.

II.

THREE times had Winter's scepter
    ruled the earth,
  And thrice been broken by the
    hand of Spring;
But by a shorter way than Nature knew
The guide Necessity was bringing forth
The woman in Ione ere her years,
And many a grace, unseen by radiant sun
Of youth and gladness, blossomed in the
    night
Of sorrow, like some lovely snow-white
    flower
That shuns the glare of daytime. When
    she passed
Along the public ways, her floating hair
And downcast, dark-fringed eyes and quiv-
    ering lips
Compelled attention; many turned about
For second glance, and murmured, "Beau-
    tiful!"

But one there was, the proud Neocritus,
High-priest of great Diana, whose bold gaze
Respected not her shrinking. Openly
He led a righteous life, but down beneath
Lay smouldering an evil, passionate heart,
Whose fires flamed red in secret. But few
          dared
A whisper of dark deeds supposed or
          known,
Because the priest was powerful; his com-
          mand
A law supreme. Many a priestess fair
Serving within the temple, was the tool
Or partner of his sin. And having marked
Ione's beauty, all his varied arts
Of soft persuasion were arrayed to win
The maiden to this virgin company,
As the lithe serpent seeks to lure the bird
With fiery, flashing eyes and graceful coils,
Till the poor victim flutters helplessly,
The strange, wild fascination having dulled
The sense of danger.

But Ione's soul
Beheld unceasingly the mother's face
Through mist of tender memory; father's
    age
And sister's youth required her loving care,
And one she saw in dreams, she doubted
    not
Would some day come again. Besides she
    felt
A vague, unreasoning fear, and strong dis-
    like
As often as she met Neocritus.
Yet answer absolute she dared not give,
And trembling, pleaded longer time for
    thought,
Whereat the priest, though chafing inwardly,
Forebore to press his purpose ; better far
A future favorite than present slave !

One day Ione, with a heavy heart,
Was passing listlessly along the way
To some secluded spot, when brokenly
A sound of reading reached her, and the
    voice,

Low-toned at first, yet thrilled exultingly,
As if the reader felt a climax come, —
A fair, white dayspring, — and his waiting
        soul
Rose like a lark to meet it.   Drawing near
The open door, she listened eagerly : —

"I would not have you to be ignorant,
Brethren, concerning them that are asleep,
So that ye sorrow not, as others do
Which have no hope."
                ("Ah !" sighed Ione, "I
Am   one   of   those;   what   hope   can   come
        to   me ?")
Again   she   listened : —
                    "For the Lord himself
Shall   come   down   out   of   heaven   with   a
        shout,
The voice of the archangel, and the trump
Of God; thereat the dead in Christ shall
        first
Arise, then we which are alive shall all
Be caught up in the clouds to meet the Lord
And be forever with him !"

Here she turned
And swiftly walked away with burning
face.
Surely this was the Christian sect, despised
By all her people, — in her father's words,
"A Galilean folly, far beneath
The least attention of a thoughtful Greek!"
She did not know that, years before, the
flame
Of Christian zeal had spread from house to
house,
Kindled by PAUL, nor that the words were
his
Which she had heard repeated; but they
glowed
Within her like the morning star in heaven,
Distant and cold, yet hinting warmth and
cheer.
"Great words," she mused, "yet meaning-
less to me.
Who are 'the dead in Christ,' and how can
they
Be raised by any power this poor sect
knows?

Nay, I am but a foolish child to think
On such delusions; none can raise the
    dead ! "

But still the music of that noble voice
Lingered within her memory; and a wish
That somehow all might be as she had
    heard
Drew her, almost unconsciously, again
Some days thereafter, to the same low
    door,
Trembling with shame, though hungering
    for a hope.

An influence all unguessed was guiding her
In ways mysterious to learn of Him,
The All-sufficient One, whose infinite heart,
Forgetting none of heaven's vast multi-
    tudes,
Twined round our little earth when time
    began,
And in far Eden breathed the breath of life
Immortal into man, forevermore, —
Almighty Love, whose everlasting arms,

That hold the whirling universe in place,
Are always underneath the fainting souls
Of all that seek Him, so that none may sink
Into eternal darkness, asking light.

The reading was in progress as she reached
The Christian's house, and swiftly glanced
    around
For watchful, curious eyes. Save for herself
The narrow street was now deserted quite,
And reassured she listened. Smooth and
    calm,
In quiet dignity, the reader's words
Flowed like a steady, sunlight-cleaving
    stream : —

" God that hath made the world, and all
    therein,
Seeing that he is Lord of heaven and earth,
Doth not inhabit temples made with hands ;
Neither can he be worshipped with men's
    hands,
As if he needed aught, for he hath given
To all the breath of life, and all things else,

And made all nations of one common blood,
To dwell on all the earth, and hath ordained
The times before appointed, and their bounds,
That they should seek the Lord, if haply
    thus
In feeling they might find him, though
    he be
Not far from every one of us, because
In him we live and move; in him we
    have
Our being, — as your poets also say:
For we are all his offspring. Therefore,
    since
Mankind is sprung from God, we ought not
    think
That Deity is like to graven gold,
Silver, or stone, in forms devised by man.
God hath allowed these times of ignorance,
But now commands repentance everywhere,
Because a day hath been appointed when
The world shall all be judged in righteous-
    ness
By one ordained thereto, in sign of which
He raised him from the dead."

Ione stood
Lost in a maze of thought, and scarcely
    heard
Beyond the strange, new words, " We ought
    not think
That Deity is like to graven gold,
Silver, or stone, in forms devised by man."
That ancient image in the temple came,
So she had learned, from mighty Zeus
    himself,
Descending through the clouds, in the dim
    dawn
Of Asian history; who knew if this
Were truth or not? If not, and man had
    formed
The statue, was it not the poor, weak
    dream
Of some old artist? Never help had come
In answer to her prayers for strength and
    light
From Artemis; had any ever seen
In very truth the high, immortal gods?
Did they exist at all, save in the mind
Of man, their maker?

While she stood, confused
With new-born doubts, the little company
Had closed their service with a hymn of
    praise,
And now came forth. But yet she heeded
    not,
Until a touch aroused her; terrified
She turned, and met the frank, inquiring
    eyes
And gentle question of Alcæus, "Child:
Art thou in trouble? Let the tender Christ
Bear all thy burdens, and uplift thy soul!"

As when the icy bonds of fountains melt,
Touched by the morning sunshine, all her
    pride
Dissolved beneath the sudden sympathy,
And the dry valley of her spirit filled
To overflow with rush of tears released.

At this he led her to a seat within
The little room, and waited for a space
Before proceeding; then with questions kind
He learned her history.

Some sixty years
Of earthly life Alcæns knew, and yet
Few were the signs of care or weariness;
A steadfast peace dwelt ever in his eyes,
And as he talked with her a heavenly smile
Hovered about his lips, or glorified
At one swift radiance all the upturned face.
Long time they sat there, while the western
 sun
Began to gather up his golden robes,
And on her spirit fell a strange, sweet calm,
As if the Christ had whispered, " Peace, be
 still ! "

At length she rose to go. Taking her hand
With all a father's tenderness, he said :
" Child, if thy mother never knew the
 Christ,
For lack of opportunity, and yet
Was heedful of his voice within her heart,
Unconscious whence it came, I may not
 doubt
That she has passed through death to
 Paradise.

For 'how shall they believe on him of
    whom
They have not heard?' So says the apostle
    PAUL,   .
And underneath the words I seem to hear
The heart-beats of the Father's infinite love
And perfect justice sound in harmony.
Nay, more, — one day our Master met a
    man
Blind from his birth, and asking not for
    faith,
Put clay upon his eyes; then bade him
    wash
Within a certain pool, and when he saw,
Declared himself the Son of God, whereat
The man believed and worshipped. And
    I know
That one so patient with the earthly eyes,
In days when he was in the flesh, is not
Less tender to the feeble sight of souls,
Now that he reigns in glory. But to thee
He giveth more of grace, and stands re-
    vealed
To-day in all his beauty; thou hast heard

His words of endless life ; believe in him
And be at rest and peace forevermore !
But yet I would not leave thee unaware
Of coming trials, for my uncle heard
The great apostle say that grievous wolves
Should, after his departure, enter in
Among us, sparing not the flock.   The
    words
May mean that we must seal our faith with
    death,
Even as others ; yet remember this, —
Our light affliction for a moment is,
And worketh out a far exceeding weight
Of everlasting glory.   Let thy thought
Dwell on these things, and come to us
    again
The first day of the week, when thou shalt
    learn   .
More of the Saviour ; meantime, fare thee
    well ! ''

So through the twilight haze Ione went,
Slowly and wondering, to her home, and
    found

The place astir with news of Marius,
Centurion of a company, on the way
To Ephesus, to aid the garrison.
And while with various thoughts her heart
    beat fast,
And flushed her face, and sometimes came
    a smile
To eyes and lips, as in the former days,
The father watched her, half in bitterness,
And murmured to himself, "Youth soon
    forgets!"
But rarely did he ask her of her life,
And seldom had she gone to him for help
Or counsel since the day her mother died,
Because his grief absorbed him. So her
    thoughts
Throughout the week were surging to and
    fro;
But one grand purpose, like a steady ship,
Faint on the far horizon, grew more clear
And bright and high, as o'er the sea it
    came,
Though lashed by winds of fear and chilly
    rain,

With waves of doubt strong dashing at the
    prow,
Till calmer water at the port it reached,
And in a morning fair, with breezes sweet,
Dropped anchor in the deep, safe harbor,
    CHRIST !

But how to tell the others of her choice,
What reasons give beyond their own, or why
She had not spoken earlier of her mind, —
Perplexed her yet ; and while she thought
    on this,
Up from the plains one sunny morn there
    came
Faint sounds of martial music, — then ap-
    peared
A rolling cloud of dust, with points of light
That circled round the roadway's nearest
    bend,
And slowly rising, thinly veiled the ranks
Of Roman soldiers, marching cityward, —
Each moment nearer, wider, more distinct,
The sunbeams breaking on their burnished
    arms

In glittering wavelets, as the rising tide
Crept onward up the slope, until at last
They reached and passed the gates, and
          formed within;
Then, while the housetops swarmed with
          eager groups,
Steadily up the street the column came,
With rhythmic step and swaying spears and
          shields
And waving plumes and ensigns gleaming
          high
And horses neighing at the trumpet call.
Familiar faces all were in the van, —
The city's garrison for many months, —
But closely following their escort marched
A company of strangers, whom all eyes
Regarded curiously; and at their head,
Mounted upon a proud, high-stepping bay,
Young Marius, a bronzed Apollo, rode,
The promise of his childhood beauty filled
To satisfaction by the ripening years;
And many knew the face, as on he passed,
And shouted friendly greeting; but the man,
Erect and flushed, impatient of delay,

Scarce seemed to hear them, while the
    column wheeled
Into a well-remembered street, and there,
Hardly a spear-cast from his hungry eyes,
Arose his boyhood's happy, care-free home,
The house of Ctesiphon ! And as he gazed,
Upon the roof appeared the household, all
Save one whose gentle face he longed to see,
The only mother that he ever knew ;
And the quick tears sprang up and veiled
    his sight,
The while they waved a welcome ; then he
    passed,
Swept onward, as it seemed, by all his men,
And blended with the throng, so fading out,
Beyond their keenest vision, as they turned
And slowly left the roof, Ione last.

How long the day that sunders waiting
    hearts !
Upon her dial-plate the shadow slept,
And Marius, chained by military cares,
Looked often to the sun, that seemed to
    stand

Still in the heavens, while a fervent heat
Bore down upon the land, until the breeze
Of morning fled away, as if in fear.
All life breathed hard, and shrank into the
   shade,
And when the day king reached his throne
   of noon
He ruled a silent city.

       Hour by hour,
High overhead the vault of dazzling blue
Shone spotless; then its base began to fade
Far to the southward, in a veil of mist,
That gathered into feathery, floating clouds,
Slow rising upward, and a whisper crept
Along the land, a message from the sea,
With promise of refreshing by and by.

At last the young centurion was released;
And in the waning of the day he sat,
Divested of his armor, at the home,
And looked again into his dear ones' eyes;
Without, a fountain in a spacious court
Plashed musically, while the whirring birds

Dipped down to drink and bathe, and scat-
      tered drops
Like diamonds round the basin. Then he
      told
Of all his life, and answered questions
      grave
From Ctesiphon, or listened to the talk
Of Lesbia and Pelope with smiles,
But ever glancing where Ione sat,
Was filled with admiration at her face,
Whose glowing eloquence was more than
      speech ;
And in his heart he whispered, " She is
      mine ! "

But while their souls were swept and stirred
      and thrilled
To strong, glad harmony by winds of love,
The sky was darkening ; glancing up they
      saw
The storm king's sable hosts arrayed for
      war, —
His fierce, impatient horses snorting fire,
Their mighty hoofs upon the firmament,

That shook beneath their trampling; then
    arose
The low, dread rumbling of his chariot
    wheels.
But in the pause that followed, suddenly
Another shadow fell across the floor,
And in the archway stood a white-robed
    form,.—
The priest Neocritus.

              Then all arose
In deference to his rank; but with a smile
Less courteous than crafty, he began
Abruptly, as he took the offered seat:
" It may surprise thee, Ctesiphon, to know
The purpose of my coming; yet I trust
That it may give thee pleasure. I have long
Looked favorably upon thine eldest child,
Because the generous gods have dowered her
With graces like Pandora's; and I deemed
Such beauty should adorn the temple courts
Of Artemis, our Lady. To this end
I oft have urged the maiden, but some
    cause —

I know not what — restrains her from the
    step ;
Wherefore I call thee to assist my words
With reasoning of thine own.   A father's
    voice
May well be more effectual than mine
In setting forth the glory of the choice
And honor of the service.   This I ask,
Not doubting of thy willingness to grant."

But Ctesiphon made answer dignified :
" Thou knowest that my daughters are the
    stay
And solace of my swift-departing days,
And surely it were better to have asked
For my consent before thou soughtest hers.
Yet think not I am one of those whose
    word
Is law unbending to a child's desire ;
Ione is of age to know her will,
And she shall have the fullest liberty
To choose her future.   Daughter, as thy
    wish
Shall be the answer, what hast thou to say ? "

Then from her seat Ione rose, and stood
Trembling and pale, but with a firm resolve
To tell them bravely of her new-gained faith.
Twice she essayed to speak, but found no
    words,
And in the glimmering, soundless lightning
    seemed
Some unsubstantial vision, as it lit
Her form and features with unearthly
    gleams ;
And Marius, shuddering, thought of those
    dim shades
That wander silent through the underworld.
At last her answer broke the stillness, low
And faltering at first, then gaining strength :

" Father, I thank thee truly, — not alone
For these, thy generous words, but for the
    love
Which thou hast always lavished. But to
    prove
My gratitude, I can but gladly take
The freedom given. And one thing I have
    done,

Sure of thy kindness, which must now be
    told ;
Some other time will serve for questioning,
Therefore I ask thy patience.

                    " Never once
Have I desired to leave thee, but have
    sought
Instead to be like sunshine in the house,
Since that dark day we all remember well ;
But mine own life was hopeless, till I
    learned
A better way of living. I have left
The ancient faith, unsatisfied, and now
Am resting on the power of One whose
    name
Is everywhere despised. And this new life
Has lifted me above all common things,
And filled me with its music ; and I feel
That far beyond our earthly days, and
    death,
Is life and joy undreamed of, peace and
    rest,
My mother, — and the Christ of Galilee ! "

She ceased; but none replied, — astonish-
  ment
Held all immovable, till Pelope,
Close nestling at her shoulder, heard a faint,
Soft whisper in the darkness of the room:
" Dear Lord, I have confessed thee! Oh, do
  thou
Remember me before thy Father's throne!"

The high-priest waited for the old man's
  word;
But Ctesiphon sat still and made no sign, —
His head bowed heavily upon his hand,
As if he heard not, saw not; whereupon
Ione spoke again, with dignity:
" Thou hast the answer, priest, — a Christian
  maid
Disdains the service of a heathen shrine!"

Neocritus arose; an angry flame
Burned in his face, and flickered in his
  voice:
" So be it, then! Doubtless thy words are
  wise,

And all the rest of Ephesus are fools,
Pleased with a toy; but yet I say to thee,
Beware the vengeance of the holy gods!
The thunderbolts of Zeus — "
                    Quick, as he spoke,
A lightning flash that tore the heavens
          wide
Blazed full upon their faces, and a crash
As if the very hills were shattered, rolled
And boomed around them. With a startled
          cry
The trembling children caught their sister's
          hands
And clung about her, Lesbia gasping, "See!
The gods are angry at thy evil choice!"
"Nay, Lesbia dear, fear not; they have no
          power
Either for good or ill." Another flash,
Another deafening peal, — and Marius stood
With folded arms and proud, uplifted head
Between the sisters and the haughty priest,
And thus addressed him: "If the gods are
          wronged,
Let them avenge the insult as they will.

Thou camest for an answer, which thou
    hast;
What further need is yet unsatisfied?"
"Young man," the priest returned, "what-
    ever else,
I need not thee to prompt me; and if thou
Dost link thy life with hers, I need not ask
For this thy rudeness greater recompense.
I go, and trust my meaning will be plain
Hereafter."
        He was gone.

             A silence fell
Upon them, deep and dread, their throb-
    bing hearts
Filled with a nameless fear. Strange whis-
    perings
Passed through the air above, as if the storm,
Uncertain how to strike, were seeking out
Each point of weakness.

            But Ione marked
That through all this her father had not
    moved;

Alarmed at length, she swiftly crossed the
    room
And knelt before him, drawing down the
    hand
That held his forehead, as she gently said,
" Dear Father, art thou angry?   Have I
    done
So wrong in this?   None loves thee more
    than I ;
Look in my face, and see ! "   He raised
    his head,
And tears bedimmed the eyes that looked
    in hers ;
A long, fond gaze ; a tender, trembling
    kiss, —
" Could I be angry with thy mother's
    child ? "

" But, father, have I done a foolish thing ? "

" I know not, dear one, save it be not wise
To cross the will of great Neocritus,
As we have done to-day.   But for thy
    faith,

Keep it, if thou art pleased ; small faith
    have I
In aught beyond my present sight and
    touch.
Sit here, my daughter, till the storm is past,
That I may feel thee near me."

                Silently
The others clustered round them.

                Far away
The murmuring voices of the upper air
Swelled to a sigh, a moan ; then with a
    roar
Weaving all lesser noises into one,
The storm came rushing on. Swiftly the
    clouds,
Spreading their banners black, joined rank
    to rank
And hurled at once their javelins thick and
    fast, —
A wild, resistless avalanche of rain ;
And all the little wandering mountain
    streams

Were swollen to foaming torrents; and the
    trees,
Lashed by the whirlwind's fury, bowed their
    heads
And groaned submission to the conqueror;
Fierce lightnings flashed incessantly, and loud
The thunder spoke in awful majesty
Unto the crouching earth; then darkness
    deep,
Like bird of evil omen, settled down,
With mighty. outstretched wings.

              Within the room
None spoke a word, till Marius' manly voice
Startled their silence: " Father Ctesiphon,
I know but little of Ione's faith,
And may not guess the meaning of this
    storm,
Unless it be a warning; but I know
That I have loved her since our childhood
    days,
And whether well or ill that she has done,
And punishment or not, I ask of her
The greatest gift that man can ever ask.

I do not fear the priest ; and if the gods
Should smite her to the earth, my only joy
Would be to die with her in my embrace
As promised wife.   If thou approvest, thus
I make request, despite the frown of Jove."

"Aye, Marius, it is well, if she consent."

"Ione, dearest, it is yea, — or nay?"

"Dear Marius," she began, with choking
          voice,
"As kind and brave as ever thou hast been,
Didst thou not know that I was always
          thine ?
I cannot give thee more than what thou hast ;
And yet thy life and mine should never
          join,
Did I not know no evil would descend
On thy dear head for aught that I have
          done.
Father, thy blessing?"
                    Kneeling at his feet
They waited for the words.

At length he sighed, —
"O unknown Powers that govern earth
    and sky
And time and life and death, if ye exist,
Be merciful! Be merciful to these
My children! Grant them golden years of
    joy,
With love new springing at each rising sun,
And intertwine the threads of life so close
That at the last the fatal Severer
May not divide them, — one in life and
    death!"
A pause, and then he said in calmer voice,
"The rain has ceased, my children; let us
    go
And from the housetop watch the clouds
    disperse."

The fresh, cool breezes fanned them in the
    face,
Freighted with delicate odors, as they stood
And saw the scattered legions of the sky
Slowly retiring, — some in sullen ranks,
While others, with a new allegiance, turned

And caught the colors of the conquering
    sun,
Flaming in gold and crimson ; and the light
Of victory and peace lay over all
The city and the plain.   White   marble
    walls,
Dripping with rain, reflected back the rays
As from a mirror ; groups of trees stood up
And   held   aloft   their   foliage,   brilliant
    green, —
Great sheaves of showery emeralds ; gardens
    fair
Arose in terraces of sparkling grass,
With fountains, gorgeous flowers and gleam-
    ing shrines ;
Above them, palaces and lofty towers
Climbed to a dizzy height, enriched and
    faced
With ivory and dazzling bronze ; below,
Like burnished shields, lay little lakes and
    pools ;
Westward, the harbor quivered restlessly,
A glowing topaz ; here the Forum shone,
Yonder the Stadium ; and the generous light

Rolled o'er the benches of the Theatre
A cataract of gold; while in the east
The Temple glittered like a mount of snow;
And round about the city curved the plain,
All gemmed with wild-flowers, as a circlet
    bright
Bent round the fair, white arm of Loveli-
    ness, —
Her shifting, shimmering veil of thinnest
    mist
Spread out, and floating, whispering to the
    sky,
" Bend lower now, and take her; she is
    thine ! "

And Marius, smiling as he read the scene,
Drew from his tunic's folds a bracelet,
    wrought
With intricate design of bird and leaf
And flower, jewelled, flashing in the light,
Clasped it around Ione's yielding arm,
And bent his head and kissed her on the
    brows.
Too happy for a word, she raised her face

With shining, moistened eyes, and tremu-
        lous lips,
And answered him in silence.

                    Long they stood,
Clasped in each other's arms.

                    The sunset paled,
And shadows deepened slowly into night,
While one by one the calm, bright stars
        appeared ;
And downward from the deep, mysterious
        sky,
Like perfume dripping from an upturned
        vase,
Softly and sweet, descended balmy rest.

III.

SWIFTLY the weeks and months had flown away,
Till once again the glad-eyed
Summer stood
Close at the threshold of her kingdom fair.
'T was early morning now upon the plains
Of Ephesus. A faint, gray mist upcurled
From Caÿster, winding slowly toward the sea
In slumbrous music, rippled by the breeze
That stole through groves of oak and tere-
    binth
And cedar, fresh and fragrant. Meadow
    flowers
Upraised their swaying, dew-filled cups,
    and smiled
To the fast paling stars, as if to say,
" O brothers, rest, and we will shine for
    you ! "
From river margin and the pearl-hung
    grass

And oleander bushes and the woods
Came twittering questions of the day's
    advance,
While glowed the east with promise, —
    amber skies
Yielding to orange, melting into gold,
Till up the gleaming pathway came the sun
In royal majesty, and touched the tops
Of Prion and Coressus, sister hills,
With magic fire; then, shooting swift and
    far
His glittering arrows, pierced the lingering
    shades.

The crisp, delicious air was vibrant now
With wakening life, and every feathered
    throat
Poured out a flood of golden melody,
And 'insects droned and chirped, while
    flocks and herds
Moved slowly toward the river pools to
    drink.
Soon city gates were opened; guards were
    changed;

Some few brown, sinewy laborers appeared
Upon the streets, with instruments of toil;
Sellers of fruits made ready for the day;
Young flower girls began to twine their
    wreaths,
And in an hour of sunrise all the town
Hummed with a varied population. Here,
Soldiers in shining armor, shaven priests,
And civil officers in trailing robes;
There, Jews of Palestine, or little groups
Of Grecian poets and philosophers;
Ladies of rank in gilded litters, borne
By stalwart men, who slowly pushed their
    way,
Elbowing active sailors from the coasts
Of Tyre and Sidon, or thin Bedouins
From lonely Petra and the wilderness;
The dwellers by Euphrates and the Nile
Mixed with the half-clad Ethiopians;
Princes, magicians, keen-eyed merchants,
    · chiefs,
Barbarians of the North, brought side by
    side
With temple servants, artists, artisans,

Musicians, perfume-mixers, burnishers,
Or stooping water-carriers, patient beasts
Of burden, and their drivers, — slaves of all
Degree and occupation crowded close
With poor and helpless ones, who idly
　　gazed
Upon the busy scene, or feebly begged
For food and coins.　The dwellers in the
　　town
Were far outnumbered by the visitors
Drawn hither by the festival and games
In honor of Diana; for the sun
Had filled the season with exuberance,
And springing grass and flowers and waving
　　wheat
And whispering leaves and opening buds
　　were held
To be bright tokens of her wondrous power
And condescension.

　　　　　　　　At the city gates
The throng divided, and the larger part
Hurried impatient to the Stadium;
Another company, with slower steps,

Passed in procession to the Temple, led
By priests and priestesses; fair Lydian
    youths
And maidens, singing soft, voluptuous airs,
Mingled with merry Phrygians, while here
Strode a Galatian warrior, yonder one
Of Cappadocia; grave, gray devotees
From all the provinces of Asia moved
In strange varieties of dress and speech,
But with one purpose, — to propitiate
The goddess for their homes.

              At length they reached
The open plain, and knelt adoringly,
While in full view the mighty structure rose.

A terraced way led to a staircase broad,
Polished and worn by countless worshippers,
And from the marble platform, smooth as
    glass,
An hundred columns reared their stately
    strength,
Massive and carved, full thirty cubits high, —
Many the gifts of kings, and others wrought

By pious hands of masters in their art.
Far up, above their graceful capitals,
Cornice and frieze and architrave spread out
Stories of strife and conquest mystical,
Crowned by a roof of gleaming marble tiles ;
And all the building throbbed with sculp-
      tured life,
Or glowed with splendid painting ; calm-
      eyed gods
And goddesses, or struggling Amazons,
Heroes and warriors ; Hermes, mighty Zeus,
Or Pallas, Heré, Artemis herself,
And Aphrodite, Eros with his bow,
Poseidon and his trident, deities
Of stream and field ·and forest ; satyrs,
      nymphs,
Or demigods, — as wondrous Herakles,
Strongest of mortals. Here a Centaur stood ;
Yonder came Tritons blowing on their
      shells ;
And all around were lions' heads, and rams,
And piled up fruit, mingled with opening
      flowers
And twining honeysuckle. Phidias,

Praxiteles, Apelles, many more,
Masters and skilful workmen; all had
    wrought
With far-famed architects, until there stood
At Ephesus the wonder of the world
And envy of all Hellas. In the midst
The statue towered high, — an image rude,
Yet reverenced more than all the glorious
    forms
By which it was surrounded. Even so
The soul of man, reaching a barren height
Unsatisfied, had waited not, but turned,
And backward traced its wandering, doubt-
    ful steps,
Till every higher faculty became
The handmaid of a lower. Grand indeed
The Temple stood, yet shrined a foolish
    faith ;
And even the lowest, meanest worshipper,
Trembling, perhaps, in superstitious fear,
Had powers greater than he gave his gods.

Rising at length, the multitude advanced,
And hours were spent in sacrifice and rites

Mysterious, — sacred dances, incense, chants,
Till after mid-day; then the priests ap-
      peared,
With all the temple servitors again,
And followed by the people, took the road
That reached the Stadium. Musicians first,
With ringing cymbals, piercing double-flutes,
And other instruments; then girls and boys,
Singing and dancing, bearing fruits and
      flowers;
And after them, Neocritus alone, —
His thick, black hair uncovered to the sun,
A stern, set face, thin lips, and flashing eyes,
And garmented in sacrificial robes,
With heavy, lustrous folds. Behind him
      marched
The priests and priestesses, in ranks that
      spread
Across the roadway, chanting high and shrill
The hymn to Artemis. And others bore
Aloft upon their shoulders images
Of gold and silver; then the surging crowd
Pressed forward shouting, joined along the
      way

By scores belated, till they reached the arch
Of entrance to the Stadium.

Then at once

The vast assemblage rose tumultuously,
And everywhere were lifted arms and scarfs,
And fluttering veils, and a great, throbbing
   roar
Of eager voices :
"Artemis !"

" Behold

Great Artemis !"
" Diana !"

" Artemis !

All Asia worships thee !"
" Diana !"

" Great

Is Artemis of Ephesus !"

And spears

And swords and shields responded with. a
   clang
That seemed to shake the building. Only
   one

In all that multitude was silent, one
Who leaned against a pillar, faint and pale
In agony of spirit, — Marius.

His men had marvelled much to see him ride
Before them on that morning listlessly,
The loose rein dropping from his nerveless
   hands,
And all unseeing where he went, his eyes
Too weary for a glance, his body drooped
In utter weakness.   Now he stood alone,
And shivered as if sickness seized him.
   Why?

Beneath his feet a dungeon lay; within,
Close crowded in the narrow, noisome place,
Were Christians; all the steadfast little
   church,
Alcæus, — and Ione !

      On the day
The high-priest left the house of Ctesiphon,
Angered that one slight girl should balk his
   power,

He planned revenge. A word dropped here
    and there,
A hint to artisans, a prophecy
Of danger should the Christians multiply
Again, as years before, at words of PAUL,
A warning that the city might decline
If reverence for Artemis should fail,
Had blown the ashes of indifference
Aside and fanned the slumbering coals of
    hate
Into a flame, till all at once a mob
Rushed to Alcæus' house in fury, dragged
The Christians forth and bound them, hurry-
    ing back
To the authorities, clamoring for their death,
Which, after consultation, was decreed,
Pending permission of the Emperor,
As fitting climax to the festival
In preparation.

              Ctesiphon had gone
With Marius impetuous to the priest,
And offered gold and jewels, — anything
To save Ione; but of no avail

Were all their efforts, — coldly he replied :
"Our Lady Artemis desires the hearts
As well as offerings, and it is her will
That all who mock her shall be put to
      death ;
Be thankful that your lives are not required,
And cease to ask for her who dared despise
Our holy faith ! ''

             All hope was over now,
Unless she should recant ; but from below
Faintly the sound of Christian hymns arose,
And Marius felt that none of them would
      yield.

No, never !   In that suffocating cave,
Darker than midnight, all were kneeling now,
Led by Alcæus in a fervent prayer.
The weary hours of day and night had
      passed
Alike to them ; the only light they had
Glared from the lions' eyes behind the bars ;
Instead of heaven's sweet winds upon the
      brow,

The hot breath of their nostrils; and they
    heard
In all the pauses of the sacred song
Deep growls of hunger. Grasping each
    other's hands
They trembled, — but a consciousness of
    power
Beyond their own upheld them.

                       Meanwhile, games
Were going on above; the wrestlers strove
And writhed for mastery, and athletes ran,
As if by Hermes sandalled, for the crown;
The pugilists, with heads and necks like
    bulls,
Rained desperate blows upon each other;
    then
Strong gladiators struggled for their lives,
With swords and nets and tridents. And
    their strife
Stirred up the people as wild beasts are
    stirred
To savagery by the taste of blood,
And all along the benches ran the words. —

A murmur, rising to an awful cry,
Hoarse and persistent, crueler than death,—
" *Bring out the Christians !* "

            Then a space was cleared
And fenced with soldiers, and an altar placed
Before a statue of the goddess, wreathed
About the base with roses ; and behind
Were ranged the priestesses, — the Asiarch
Lysanias of Smyrna in the chair
Of judgment.   Soon the prisoners were
      brought
Before him, one by one, Alcæus first.

The accusation read, Lysanias asked :
" Art thou a Christian ? "
                " Yea ! "
                " And dost thou know
The penalty ? "
          " I do."
             " What madness, man,
Has prompted thee to throw away thy life ?
Be reasonable,— curse the Christ ; that done,
I may release thee."

" Ay, thou dost not know
That he who loses life for Christ's sweet
    sake
Shall find it more abundantly. Thy power
And all thou hast is given thee from him ! "

"Take him away."

         And hurriedly they tried
The others ; but none yielded. Last of all
Ione answered to the summons. Then
The high-priest had her father brought
    within,
With Lesbia and Pelope, that all
Might suffer to the utmost, and prepared
To read the grim indictment.

         But a hand
Seized hers in shaking grasp, and in her ear
Trembled the voice of Marius, changed
    and harsh
With deadly fear, as rapidly he said :
" Ione, dearest, listen ! Leave the Christ
And call upon Diana ! Take of these,"—

Catching some jewels from a casket brought
By Lesbia, — " these ornaments of thine,
And offer on her altar for thy life !
Nay, take the bracelet, dearest, for I know
That I must give thee up in life or death;
But oh, thou must not die ! Ione — "

" Dear — "

She slowly turned her face, all wet with
     tears,
And looked him in the eyes. The throng
     around
Bent forward eagerly to catch the words:
" My Marius, dost thou tempt my soul with
     these
To leave my Master, as Iscariot did?
And even if I might, what should I care
For any life without thee? Oh, my own,
Dear father, sisters, friends, I love not life
Better than truth ! The gracious Christ I
     serve
Will raise me up again. Let all of you
Who love me learn of him, and any death
Shall only re-unite us. Marius,

Thou hast not dreamed how much I love
    thee yet;
But thou wilt know hereafter."

               Down she drooped
Her weary head, and murmured, "O my
    Lord,
I thank thee for this sudden, wondrous
    strength,
Made perfect in my weakness!"

               And a sigh
Involuntary broke from all the crowd,
As the tense bowstring, suddenly released,
Springs to its place with apprehensive thrill,
Foreseeing death in the arrow. Ctesiphon
Groaned in despair, and wrung his helpless
    hands
Convulsively; and down the sisters' cheeks
Tears fell like rain. But Marius staggered
    back,
Weak as a child, and would have fallen to
    earth
Had not a soldier stayed him.

                              Then the priest,
Unmoved, began to read the charge. But
        she —
Lifting her violet eyes above the throng,
Above the circling thousands in the seats,
Along the side of green Coressus, up
Beyond the trilling, soaring birds — at
        length
Rested in God's blue sky, while all of earth
Seemed to dissolve away. Slowly a vision
        sweet
Opened before her.

                              For a pearly cloud
That closed one gate of heaven rolled
        aside,
And a bright spirit beckoned her within, —
The mother's face and form ; but glorious
        now
In such a smile as those redeemed may
        wear !
Then, while the glad sight filled Ione's
        gaze,
And scarce a breath escaped the parted lips,

Her hands close locked, in rapture keen as
    pain,
Suddenly all the avenue was filled
With countless flashing ones, that raised
    their harps
And sang triumphantly, " *Ay, blest are they,*
The pure in heart, for they shall see their
    God! "
And others answered them afar, " *These*
    came
Out of great tribulation, and their robes
Are white and glistening; they are washed
    in blood,
Even the Lamb's, who bears away the sin
Of all the world! "

              And then a splendor burned,
Dazzling the wing-veiled angels; but she
    saw,
Even with eyelids closed, the form of One
Like to the Son of Man, with hands and
    feet
Pierced by the cross-nails; and his thrilling
    voice

Rang full and tender as the far, sweet chime
Of silver cymbals:

> "BE THOU NOT AFRAID
OF THEM THAT KILL THE BODY, AND AFTER
> THAT
HAVE POWER TO DO NO MORE, — FEAR NOT,
> MY CHILD;
I AM THE RESURRECTION AND THE LIFE,
AND THOU SHALT BE WITH ME IN PARADISE
TO-DAY!"

The Asiarch, wondering at her face,
Thrice questioned ere she heard him; then
she said,
"Yea, I am ready!" So they led her out, —
The rude, imbruted Ethiopian slaves
Awe-struck and trembling at her confi-
dence, —
And from the arena's sands of bloody death,
She, with a score of others, entered Life.

.   .   .   .   .   .

Beneath the dust of centuries there lies

A sculptured tomb of marble, with these words

Engraved upon the pavement: "IN THIS PLACE

SLEEPS IN THE PEACE OF JESUS CHRIST THE DUST

OF CTESIPHON AND IONE, SIDE BY SIDE,

FATHER AND DAUGHTER.

"BLESSED ARE THE DEAD

WHOSE DEATH IS IN THE LORD; THEY REST FROM STRIFE,

AND THEIR WORKS FOLLOW THEM.

"THIS TOMB WAS BUILT

BY MARIUS, A MINISTER OF CHRIST."

5

www.ingramcontent.com/pod-product-compliance
Lightning Source LLC
Chambersburg PA
CBHW021227260626
47172CB00002B/645